The Mud Club

Randy Powell

SCHOLASTIC INC.

New York   Toronto   London   Auckland   Sydney
Mexico City   New Delhi   Hong Kong   Buenos Aires

Illustrations
Jim Cooke

Developed by ONO Books in cooperation with Scholastic Inc.

ISBN 0-439-57918-X

3   4   5   6   7   8   9   10   23   12 11 10 09 08 07 06 05

Contents

Welcome to This Book

Do you have any old friends who have drifted away? You don't talk to them much anymore. But you just can't forget them, either.

Eden is like that for Milo. They haven't talked in years. And ever since they stopped talking, Milo's life hasn't been going that great. His car barely runs. His friend Lucy would like to be something more. But Milo isn't interested in her in that way.

Lucy thinks Milo is still hung up on Eden. And maybe he is. When Eden is missing, Milo takes up the search. What do you think he will find?

Target Words These words will help you understand what Milo and Eden are searching for.

- **flaw:** a fault or a weakness
  The Argos try to hide their flaws.
- **imitation:** a copy of someone or something else
  Milo felt like a cheap imitation of the Argos.
- **values:** a set of beliefs or ideas about what is most important
  Young people don't always have the same values as their parents.

Reader Tips Here's how to get the most out of this book.

- **Illustrations** Look at the illustration on page 9. Illustrations provide details about the characters that aren't provided in the story. What details do you notice about Milo and Lucy from the illustration that aren't contained in the text?
- **Make Inferences** Authors do not always directly tell readers everything that takes place in a story. Instead, they provide details that allow readers to figure things out for themselves. Use information from the story clues and what you already know to make a guess, or inference, about the plot or the characters' actions.

1

Lucy and Me

The Mud Club on a Saturday night? Sure, why not.

It's another Saturday night. I drive over to my friend Lucy's apartment building to pick her up.

Lucy's mom opens the door. "Hi, Milo, sweetie. How're you doing? Milo, meet my new boyfriend Vern."

Vern and I shake hands. Odd. Vern is the **spitting image** of Bill Clinton.

"You two men sit here and talk about cars or something. I'll go see where Lucykins is."

Vern and I look at each other.

I wonder if he knows what he's in for. Mrs. Del Meuth's boyfriends usually last about six weeks, give or take a weekend.

I want to tell Vern: I am not Lucy's boyfriend. Lucy and I are just friends.

"Hey, amigo," Vern says. He holds out a twenty-dollar bill.

"What?"

"Take Lucy out tonight on me." Vern winks in Mrs. Del Meuth's direction.

I look at Vern. I look at the twenty.

"Okay, amigo?"

"We're just friends," I say.

Vern chuckles. "Whatever toots your horn. Just have a good time on your old friend Vern."

I take the twenty. I admit, it's not one of my finest moments.

"Here she is!" Mrs. Del Meuth sings.

Lucy steps out of the bedroom. Vern's eyebrows hit the ceiling. Lucy's hair is a blinding shade of orange. Her stretch pants are purple and pink. Her white cowboy boots make her legs look real chubby.

—Heads Up!—

Milo tells Vern that Lucy isn't his girlfriend. How do you think Milo feels about Lucy?

"You two have fun now," Mrs. Del Meuth says. "Drive careful, Milo. Wear your seat belts. There's all kinds of crazy people out there!"

Lucy and I take the elevator down. We step outside into the parking lot. An old man is waiting at my car.

"How many times have I told you not to park that car in the loading zone! It leaks oil. Next time I see this piece of junk parked in the loading zone, I'm gonna have it towed away!"

"Why, thank you so much," Lucy says sweetly. "And you have a nice evening yourself, you hear?"

We climb into my car. The apartment manager just stands there watching us.

I turn the key. "Come on, baby," I say.

The starter grinds and grinds. Gas **fumes** fill the car. The manager is shaking his head back and forth.

Finally, it starts. I rev it a few times.

"You know, Milo," Lucy says. "I just have a feeling something good is going to happen to us tonight."

"It just did," I say. "My car started."

Lucy says, "I just have a feeling something good is going to happen to us tonight."

It's a typical scene at the Mud Club. The Mud Club is a dance club for people twenty-one and under. There's a line of freaky-looking people waiting to get in. Folks on the **fringes** of life. Lucy and I fit right in.

We get to the front of the line. "Oh, no, I forgot," Lucy says. "I'm broke."

"No problem," I say. "Here."

I dig into my front pocket. I hand Lucy the crumpled twenty that Vern gave me.

"What's this?"

"Just keep it."

"What did you do, raid your piggy bank?"

Inside, music and dancing and flashing lights fill the whole room. People dip their hands into big buckets of mud. They paint the mud on their faces. When the mud dries, it makes a mask. The mask hides your **flaws.** It's like being **airbrushed.**

---**Heads Up!**-----------------

Look up fringe *in the glossary. How does it help describe the people at the Mud Club?*

10

Lucy always sticks close to me when we go out. She doesn't like to be left alone. One time we were at another club. This guy came up to her and said, "Man, you are one ugly chick."

She still hasn't gotten over that.

Lucy is seventeen, a year younger than I am. We've been friends all through high school. She's one of the funniest people I know. But she's pretty sad, too. She once told me that she doesn't really like herself. I wish there was something I could do to help her be happy.

I think she wishes that for me, too.

2

Mrs. Argo

Talk about a blast from the past.

The band is taking a break. The lights are on. Lucy and I are people-watching.

One guy keeps walking by us, eyeing Lucy. He looks eighteen or nineteen. The mud on his face is painted to look like a skull mask.

"Scary," Lucy **mutters** to me.

Someone catches my eye. There's a lady at the far end of the room. She looks completely out of place. But she also looks familiar, very familiar.

"No way. I don't believe it," I say.

"What, what, what?" Lucy asks. She checks out where I'm looking. "Who, that soccer mom? Nice tan."

"It's Mrs. Argo," I say quietly.

"Mrs. Argo looks fresh off the cover of _Good Housekeeper_ magazine," Lucy says.

"I think you mean *Good Housekeeping*," I say. But my mind's on Mrs. Argo. "She's an old friend of my parents. That's Eden's mom. I've told you about Eden."

"Ooh, Eden!" Lucy says, excited. "Your old girlfriend."

"I've told you before, she wasn't my girlfriend."

"Milo, let's go over and talk to her mother."

"What?"

"Come on, let's see what she's doing here." Lucy tugs at my arm.

"Just hold on a second." I yank my arm from her. A bit too hard.

Lucy looks away. She knows me too well. She has just read my mind. I don't want Mrs. Argo seeing me with somebody like Lucy.

How come I still care what Eden's mother thinks of me? It used to matter a lot. It used to matter to my parents, too. It was like a big game. Let's try to be like the Argo family. But not anymore. That game had ended.

The music starts back up. It's trance music. People in the crowd start to sway and spin to the haunting music.

Lucy starts getting into it. She's got her arms in the air. Her eyes are closed. Her bracelets are jangling. Lucy may be chubby, but she's a great dancer.

The skull-face guy is back. He circles Lucy. He dips his hand into a small pot of mud.

Lucy still has her eyes closed. I see her open one eye for a second and take a peek. I'm trying to keep track of where Mrs. A is.

Lucy grabs my sleeve. "Don't go," she says.

"I'm . . . uh . . . not."

"I mean it. Don't leave me alone here with Mr. Trick or Treat."

"He won't bother you."

"He does bother me. He *is* bothering me."

"Look, I'll be back in two minutes."

"Milo, NO!"

Skull Man is right up in Lucy's face. He has to stand on his toes. He's doing this freaky dance. He's pushing his head in and out like a chicken. Yeah, he's doing the old chicken dance.

Lucy is still clutching my sleeve. I pull my arm free and head across the room. I tell myself Lucy will be fine. But I'm afraid to look back.

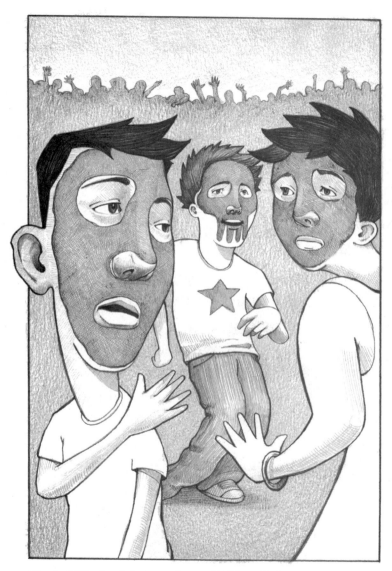

"Look, I'll be back in two minutes," Milo tells Lucy.

I quickly wipe the mud off my face. I go up to Mrs. Argo. She gives me a quick glance and looks away. Then she looks back at me. A light goes on in her face.

"Milo?" She brings her hand up to her mouth. "It can't be! Milo!"

I feel my face blushing underneath the last of the mud.

Mrs. A tries to talk over the music, but it's too loud. She motions for me to follow her. We go out into the hallway. It's crowded out here. People are sitting on the floor or leaning against the wall. We find a space against the wall. We're right between two couples making out.

"I cannot believe how much you've grown, Milo! It's been almost four years!"

Mrs. A's voice seems to carry for miles. People turn and look at us and **snicker.** Mrs. A isn't bad looking for being close to fifty. I can't tell if people think she's my mother or my girlfriend. I don't know which is more embarrassing.

She asks me how I am, how's my family, and all that. But I can tell she's hardly listening to my answers.

"How's Eden?" I finally ask.

Mrs. A's face changes. She leans closer to me. I catch a whiff of mint. But underneath, I can still smell the coffee breath.

"Actually, I was hoping you might have seen her," Mrs. A says. "Have you?"

I shake my head no.

"Milo . . . could we go and talk? There's a little coffeehouse across the street."

"I guess so," I say. "I'll have to go tell my friend. I'll meet you over there."

But Mrs. A is already halfway to the exit. She doesn't bother to look back. She just expects that I'll drop everything and follow. That's typical.

Heads Up!

How would you describe Mrs. Argo? What do you learn about her in this chapter?

3

Eden Takes Off

And why should I care?

I head back to the dance floor. I look around for Lucy. It's hard to see, though. The lights are flashing. All the faces are covered in mud.

I give up and go to the exit. I get my hand stamped. Outside, it has started to rain. The sidewalk is glazed and the night sky is thick with clouds. I head across the street to the coffeehouse.

"Eden left home. It's been about five days," Mrs. A tells me after I sit down. "There was no warning. She didn't have any problems. She was right on track, heading for graduation this spring. And then she just left. She left us a note. It said she needed to get away for a while. That was it. She didn't take her car. Her father and I bought her a BMW six months ago, you know."

I fight the urge to roll my eyes.

"Not a brand-new BMW, mind you. It's used."

I want to tell her, You want to see used? Come on out and take a look at my car. Now *that's* used.

A bunch of memories are coming back to me. The Argos were the perfect family. They had two perfect kids who never gave their parents any worries. The airbrushed Argos. And my parents always wanted to be just like them. They were Argo wanna-bes. But my parents were never really good enough for that. And I was never good enough for Eden.

"Of course, we called all her friends," Mrs. A went on. "We called the police. But she's eighteen. They couldn't do much but report her as missing. There's been no trace—"

"You didn't call me," I say.

Mrs. A looks at me, startled. It's like she's thinking, Is he joking? Did he ever really think he was Eden's friend? Is he that big a fool?

"No," she says. "We didn't call you."

I look out the window at the street.

After a while Mrs. A says, "I'm so worried. What if some **lunatic** is holding her prisoner?

Suppose he had a knife and made her write that note?" She brings her hands to her throat. I notice how tanned they are, how her rings sparkle. She takes a deep breath.

"But last night, we had a **breakthrough.** One of her friends called me. She said a friend of a friend saw Eden a few days ago. She was at this Mud Club place. She was seen with someone called Meat."

"Meat?" I say.

"Yes. Do you know anybody called *Meat*?"

I shake my head.

"I came here just to see if anyone's heard of this Meat person," she says.

"I'm not a regular here," I say. "But I know a few people who are regulars. Maybe I could go back and ask around."

"Oh, Milo, would you? I wasn't getting anywhere. Everyone was looking at me like I was a . . . a . . ."

"Soccer mom?"

She smiles weakly. "Yes, that's right."

As I get up to go, she touches my arm. "Keep in touch, Milo."

"Do you know anybody called *Meat*?" Mrs. Argo asks Milo.

Back in the club, the place is still packed. The music is **throbbing.** The crowd is rolling and swelling like the ocean.

I'm not thinking about Eden or Meat right now. I spend the next twenty minutes looking for Lucy but have no luck.

I head out to the lobby. I run into a girl I know named CQ. She's using her shirt to wipe the mud off her wing-tip glasses.

"Hey, CQ," I say. "You seen Lucy anywhere in the last hour?"

CQ squints at me. She puts her glasses on.

"Milo! How's it going?" She's still got specks of mud on her glasses. "Yeah, I did see Lucy. Is she nuts?"

"You saw her?"

"Yeah, like maybe forty minutes ago. She was with this freaky dude. His face was all painted like a skull. She took off with him."

"With *that* guy?"

"Yeah. I saw them go out the side door. His motorcycle was parked out there. They got on it and blazed outta here."

"You're sure? Maybe they're coming back."

"Nope. I heard somebody call to him, 'Hey Meat, don't you guys want to get your hands stamped?' But he just—"

"What? What did you say? Did you say his name was *Meat*?"

"Yeah. Meat. I'm like, yucko, Meat? Hey, Milo, wanna go back and get some more mud?"

Heads Up!

What do you think happened to Lucy?
What would you do if you were Milo?

Golden Girl

Eden and me? It was never meant to be.

I come up with a plan. I'll drive back to Lucy's apartment. I'll stake out the place. I'll wait for this Meat guy to bring Lucy home. That is, if he brings her home. Oh, God. He has to bring her home.

I flip on what's left of the wipers. They scream and scream and scream.

I park in the back of the parking lot instead of the loading zone. It would be just my luck to have the manager come squawking at me.

Time goes slowly. I keep yawning. I look at my watch. Twelve-forty. One o'clock. One-fifteen. There's plenty of time to sit and think.

Think about Eden.

She was what you'd call a high **achiever.** She went to private school. She was completely out of my league. But a long time ago our parents used to be friends. So Eden and I spent a lot of time together as kids.

When we were ten, she took me into her playhouse in her backyard. She wanted to show me her collection. She was so proud of it. It was a bunch of washed-up objects she'd found on beaches. There was stuff like a seal skull, a doll's head, a Korean tennis shoe, a fancy motorcycle seat, all kinds of glass bottles.

"What do you do with all this stuff?" I had asked her.

"What do you do with any collection?" she said. "You show it off, of course. Don't you collect anything?"

I shook my head. Once again I felt like a big zero compared to Eden Argo.

When we became teenagers, I had visions of kissing her in that playhouse. It would have been

―Heads Up!―

Why do you think this chapter is called "Golden Girl"?

the perfect place, with the rain tapping on the roof. There were times when I really felt like it might happen. But I couldn't get up the nerve to make the first move.

One time our families went skiing together for a whole week. My parents were really excited. They had made it into the Argos' inner circle. They were finally good enough. Eden and I were fourteen. We spent most of the week together. I was getting good vibes from her. We would sit and talk in front of the fire. She would look right into my eyes.

One night, we were in the hot tub in our bathing suits. There we were, looking up at the snow falling. We were up to our necks in jet bubbles. I drifted closer to her. This was my chance. Don't think about it, I told myself. So I grabbed her. I started kissing her. She pushed me away. After that, I couldn't even look at her.

Her parents didn't invite my parents over anymore. I wondered if it had something to do with me. Eden was busy with her life in private school. I only saw her one more time. I was riding my bike along a trail with a friend of mine. It was a Sunday afternoon. Suddenly, there was Eden. She was walking. I was on my bike. She saw me and stopped. She waited for me to catch up. She was smiling at me. When I got close, I heard her say, "Milo, I haven't seen you for a while and I just wanted to . . ."

I didn't stop. My friend said, "Hey, that girl was trying to talk to you." But I didn't answer. I just kept riding, right past her.

Pound pound pound.
Pound pound pound pound pound.
I open my eyes.
Something is pounding on my window.
It's a fist.
Pound pound pound.
I jump and straighten up. I try to focus my eyes. I look at my watch, then outside. A man is pounding on my window. It looks like Bill Clinton. The former President of the United States wants me to roll down my window.

I look at my watch again. Then I blink my eyes about five times. It's three in the morning. I've been asleep in my car for almost two hours.

I roll down my window.

"What are you still doing here?" It's Vern.

"Huh?"

"Wake up, amigo."

"So did . . . Lucy come home?" I ask.

"Hours ago. So what are you still doing here?"

"She's home? Lucy's all right?"

"What are you, some kind of a half wit?"

"You got that right," I answer.

Vern shakes his head and walks away. And my car, by some miracle, starts up first try.

─**Heads Up!**─────────

Milo and Eden haven't seen each other in four years. Why not?

5

Meeting Meat

Maybe Skull Face isn't such a bad guy.

"How was your date with Lucy last night?" my mom asks in the morning.

"It wasn't a date," I say.

"Okay . . . whatever. Didn't you go dancing together last night?"

"We don't 'dance'," I say. "We just, kind of, get into the music."

"Oh. When are we going to get to meet this Lucy, anyway?"

I pretend I didn't hear that.

After a while Mom says, "So . . . did anything interesting or exciting happen?"

Hah. What if I told her the news about Eden? I wonder what she and my dad would think. My parents were always comparing me to the Argo kids. All I ever heard was, "Peter and Eden are such good students. Peter and Eden are so polite. Peter and Eden listen to their parents. Can't you at least try to be more like Peter and Eden?"

Oh, I tried all right. I tried for years. But the harder I tried, the more I realized I'd never come close. I'd always be a cheap **imitation.** Why bother trying? It was easier just to give up.

Well, maybe the airbrushed Argos are not so perfect. Maybe that's why Eden ran off. Maybe they had cracks in their masks.

"Nothing happened," I say to my mom. "Same old Saturday night."

And I leave it at that. I can't say anything more to my parents. I'd like to. But it's just too late.

Later, I go over to Lucy's. The chicken-dance guy is there. They're sitting on the couch. He's got his arm around Lucy. She explains that his real name is George.

Heads Up!

Milo says the Argos might have "cracks in their masks." What does he mean?

The only people who call him "Meat" are his motorcycle buddies.

Lucy's face is glowing.

I can't tell what this guy is all about. Is he a true gentleman? Or is he some kind of crazy person who has been keeping Eden in a cage in his basement?

I ask him how he got the nickname Meat.

"Well," he says, chuckling. "Me and a bunch of my motorcycle friends went into this Greek restaurant. I ordered meat. And the Greek waiter, he asks me if I'd like my meat on a shish kebab. You know, meat on a stick. So anyway, I say, 'No, I'd like it on a dish kebab.'" George bursts out laughing at his own joke.

Lucy starts laughing, too.

"You should have seen my friends," George says. "They fell on the floor. I spit you not."

"That is priceless," Lucy says.

I am puzzled. "So that's when they started calling you Meat?"

"From that day forward."

"Why 'Meat'? I mean, why didn't they call you 'Dish'? Or 'Kebab'? Or 'Greek'?"

George looks at me. Then he turns to Lucy. "We'd better be going," he says.

Lucy nods. She says to me, "George and I are going for a ride on his motorcycle."

I'm not sure I like Lucy's attitude. Overnight she's turned into this guy's girlfriend. She's acting like I don't even matter.

"What happened last night?" I say to Lucy. "Why'd you ditch me?"

She ignores my question. Instead she turns to George and says, "Actually, last night Milo dumped me for a hot soccer mom."

That reminds me. I'm supposed to find out about Eden. So I ask George, "Do you know a girl named Eden? Someone saw you together."

"Why are you so interested?"

"Eden and I go back a long way," I say. "Our parents used to be friends. But I haven't seen her for almost four years."

"Why's that?"

"I did something stupid."

George thinks about this for a moment. "What if I told you Eden's a friend of mine? What would you want to know?"

For starters, how could she possibly be a friend of someone like you? That's what I'm **tempted** to say. I'd almost find it more believable if he told me he had Eden locked in his basement.

Instead I say, "I'd be curious to know where she is. And why she left home the way she did."

"Would you run and tell her parents?"

"Not if Eden didn't want me to."

George smiles. "That's the right answer."

"Actually, I'd like to see her," I say.

"Sorry to interrupt here," Lucy says, "but I need to know something, George. Are you and Eden friends?"

George looks at her. "Yes."

"What do you do, hang out at the Mud Club to meet girls?"

"You're the only one I've met at *that* club," George says.

"Boy do I feel special," Lucy says.

George takes her hand and gets all serious. "I'm not looking anymore. Not anywhere. I want you to trust me. And I want to get to know you. I want to know you better than I've ever known anybody. Better than I even knew my dog. He's

Maybe George has a good heart. Maybe he'll be good to Lucy.

dead, by the way. Good old Rex. He got run over by a tractor. Twice."

"I was really getting into your speech until the part about the dog," Lucy says.

I clear my throat to show them I'm still in the room. Plus, I'm sort of wondering how that could happen. How could a healthy dog get nailed, not once but twice, by a piece of heavy farm equipment?

I'm also thinking that maybe this George has a good heart. Maybe he'll be good to Lucy. She hasn't had much luck with guys. Most people just don't treat her with respect. I've been a little guilty of that myself. So maybe he's all right. Maybe George really did help Eden out.

George leans toward me. "If you really want to see Eden, I'll have to go talk to Wayne."

"Who's Wayne?"

"He's the guy who knows where Eden is. He'll find out."

"Find out what?"

"Whether Eden wants to see you."

Heads Up!

Describe George. Do you think that Milo should be worried about him or not?

6

Action Figures

I'm no superhero. What did I get myself into?

Over a week goes by. It's almost April. I go to school during the day. I work as a busboy clearing tables in the evenings.

Then Thursday night, Lucy calls me.

"It's a go," she says. "Come over Saturday morning and pick us up."

I go tell my mom I'll be gone Saturday. She says there are no chores to get done. I'm free and clear.

"Got a minute?" she asks me.

"Sure."

"Milo, you didn't tell me you saw Dolly Argo last week."

"How did you—?"

"She called while you were at work. She said she's been waiting for you to call her. Are you going to call her?"

"Yeah."

"Tonight?"

"I guess."

"Dolly and I had a long talk. We haven't talked for over a year. She told me about Eden. How come you didn't tell Dad and me that Eden had disappeared like that?"

"I don't know. I really don't."

Mom considers this for a moment then asks, "Any leads?"

"I think so."

"Is that what you're doing Saturday?"

"Yeah."

Mom nods. She starts to say something. Then she takes a deep breath. Finally she just says what all mothers are **programmed** to say.

"Just promise me that you won't do anything dangerous, will you please?"

I call Mrs. Argo.

"Did you find this Meat person?" she asks.

"I can't tell you that."

"Why not?"

"I just can't."

"Does he want money? Tell him I'll pay him."

"No, no one said anything about money, Mrs. Argo. But I'll know more after Saturday."

"All right," she says. "Just don't keep me in the dark, Milo. Please. Will you check in with me as soon as you know anything? Promise me, Milo! Will you?"

"Okay, I promise."

Saturday morning, I pick up George and Lucy. My car keeps dying at stoplights. It's belching clouds of purple smoke.

"Your **chariot** seems to be running a bit rough," George says.

"Yeah."

"Have you checked the points and plugs lately?" he asked.

"Checked the what and what?"

"Oh, Lord."

─Heads Up!─

Describe Milo's car. What can you learn about Milo from the way he treats his car?

George directs me to a neighborhood east of downtown Seattle. I've never been there before. We get out and walk. Most of the shops have gone out of business. Homeless men and women are camped out on the sidewalks.

We come to a shop on one of the side streets. The shop is called Action Figures. And that is what it's full of. There are action figures from TV shows, horror movies, rock bands, cartoons, you name it. There are shelves of different Bruce Lee's. There's Spiderman, Batman, and all their many enemies. There's a military section. There are sports figures and female action figures. But there aren't any Barbie dolls. A big man with a bushy beard is peering out the window.

"Is Eden here?" I ask him.

"If she were, she'd be busted," the man says. He's still looking out the window.

"What do you mean?"

He signals for me to come to the window. "See that woman out there walking the dog?"

"Yeah?"

"If she's not a private detective, I'll eat my underwear," he says.

"No way."

"See how she's looking over here real casual like? She's a pro. She parked her car down the block. She thinks you've led her to Eden. But we're going to slip out the back door. I've got my motorcycle parked down the alley."

"Uh . . . motorcycle?" I say.

"You got a problem with motorcycles?"

"What about my car?"

"We'll let the private eye keep an eye on your car. Eden wants to see you. I'm going to take you. By the way, I'm Wayne."

"Eden really wants to see me?" I say as I shake Wayne's hand.

I look out the window again at the lady. "Man," I say. "I didn't even notice her."

"Well, I guess Eden's parents can afford to hire the best."

"So, how did you know they'd have me followed here?"

"I didn't. Eden did. I guess she knows her parents pretty well."

Wayne starts to head for the back door.

"Wait a sec. What about George and Lucy?"

I'd almost forgotten they were here. They're standing close together. They look like a nice couple. Weird, but nice.

"Don't worry about us," George says. "We'll hold down the fort."

"I owe you," I say. "Both of you."

"Get going," Lucy says, smiling. "I have a feeling something good's going to happen."

Heads Up!

Wayne is about to take Milo to see Eden. What do you think Milo is going to find?

7

Road to Eden

Finally, I get the story. Well, most of it.

The first few miles, I hang onto this Wayne guy. I'm scared out of my pants. I keep thinking we're going to pop a wheelie. We lean together on the turns. It seems like we're going to scrape the pavement. I've never felt anything like this in my life. The rush of wind is awesome. It's like I'm flying. It's totally different than being in a car. There are no windows or roof. Just a slow-moving open sky and a blur of pavement.

Wayne pulls into a supermarket to get some supplies. We're way out of town by now. I go into the store with him.

"How do you know Eden, anyway?" I ask him.

"Long story," he says.

"I've got time."

At first, Milo is scared. But then he begins to enjoy the ride.

"Okay. First, we'll pick up a couple of things and have a bite to eat."

So that's what we do. There's a field across the street. Some kids are having baseball practice there. We sit down at a picnic table. Then Wayne tells me how he met Eden.

It was six months ago, he says. That's when she came into his shop. It was pouring rain outside. She was soaked. He could tell she didn't belong in that neighborhood. She seemed lost and sort of dazed.

"She's staring at all the action figures," Wayne says. "She's picking them up. We talk a little. She said she'd parked her car a few blocks away. She was taking a walk around the neighborhood. Said she used to do some volunteer work at the food bank down the street. She'd walked by my shop a few times. But she'd never come in. Not till that day," he says.

Wayne takes a bite of his sandwich and chews. He watches the baseball players for a minute. Then he continues.

"I made her some tea. She stayed all afternoon. She talked and I listened. She was lost, all right.

In more ways than one. She said she needed to break out of her life. I told her, 'You ain't breaking out of anything, kid. Go home. You'll snap out of it.' And she left.

"But a few Sundays later, there she was again. She started coming by pretty often. A lot of teenagers do that. They come to my action figure shop and just talk. They feel safe there. And that's what Eden did. She met George and some of the other regulars. She met some street kids. They talked about life and everything under the sun.

"Then one day she comes in all excited. This was about two weeks ago. She's got a knapsack. She says she finally did it. She just left home. I figured she had some big fight with her parents."

I just sit there nodding at all this.

"So I told her, look, you better go home and work it out. She said, 'No, it wasn't a fight. I'm not doing this out of anger. I've thought it out. I left my car, my computer, my books, everything. It's my birthday today. I'm 18. This is my present to me. It's time to grow up.' She wanted a place to get away and . . . figure things out. I told her I knew just the place."

"What place?" I ask. "Where are we going?"

"You'll see soon enough," he says. "We better get a move on."

"Is Eden all right?" I ask.

Wayne **hesitates.** He looks straight at me. "Maybe. How about you?"

We finish our sandwiches in silence. Then we're back on the motorcycle. We're heading west, toward the ocean.

Heads Up!

Milo asks if Eden is all right. Wayne says "Maybe. How about you?" What do you think Wayne means?

8

Reunion

It's been four years.
I don't even know Eden anymore.

An hour or so later, we're traveling through heavy forest. We turn at an unmarked dirt road. We go another five miles or so. It's really bumpy. Mud puddles are everywhere.

We park next to a car and a small motorcycle. Wayne takes the two grocery bags out of his **saddlebags.** We start off down a trail. Pretty soon we come to a cabin. A couple of little kids are out front. They're playing with action figures. They wave to Wayne and keep on playing.

Two women are sitting in chairs on the porch. One is Wayne's sister. The other is Eden. She smiles a bit **awkwardly** when she sees me. She gets up and lays her book on the chair.

A few minutes later, Eden and I are walking along a wooded path.

"Nice place here," I say.

"Yeah. It's Wayne's sister's place. I've been helping with chores and baby-sitting."

The trail opens up, and there's the Pacific Ocean. I take a deep breath. I can smell the sand and **driftwood.** The wind is steady. I watch the waves roll in and break, one after another.

We sit down on a log.

"Whatever happened to that collection of yours?" I ask. "All that washed-up beach stuff."

"I got rid of that a long time ago," she says.

"All of it? Even the seal skull?"

"It was just a bunch of trash," she says.

She stretches her legs out in front of her. I steal a look at her face. She has beach cheeks. They're **ruddy.** That's it. And her face is glowing. It reminds me of Lucy's face the other day.

Heads Up!

Eden's face looks like Lucy's to Milo. What do their faces tell you about how they feel?

Eden catches me staring at her and smiles. "You went to a lot of trouble to find me."

"It wasn't that much trouble. Well, yes it was. Kind of."

"It was nice of you. I didn't think you cared. What else have you been up to lately?" she asks. "For the past four years."

"Not much."

"How's your family?"

"Fine. Aren't you going to ask me how your parents are?"

She looks out at the ocean.

"How come you haven't contacted them?" I ask. "You could save them a lot of worry."

Still she says nothing.

"Well, how come you left home then?" I ask her. "Or is it none of my business?"

"How come I left home? Because I didn't like what I was turning into."

"What were you turning into?"

"I'm sure you could see it even four years ago. But I'll give you a nice juicy example. Six months ago, I decided I had to have a BMW."

"Wow. So did I," I say.

"Very funny," she says. "Did your parents buy you one? My parents bought me one. Poof. Eden gets what she wants, yet again. I think maybe the second time I was driving it, I had this vision of myself. And it really did scare me. I started blaming my parents. It's all their fault. They've made me into this spoiled monster."

"So you took off?" I said.

She nods. "I wrote them this really awful letter. I told them what a great big fake their life is. How everything they do is for show. How their **values** are all screwed up. Oh, I thought I was really being honest for a change.

"But then I decided that I was just being mean and selfish. I didn't want to hurt them. I tore up the letter. I left them a quick note instead. I know I'll have to explain it all to them, **eventually.** When I go back. I don't know if I'll ever get them to understand it all."

Heads Up!

What kind of person was Eden turning into? Why didn't she like herself?

"Maybe it's not your job to make them understand," I say. "Maybe all you can do is tell them what you're thinking and feeling. Maybe you could just leave it at that?"

Eden gives me a serious look and nods. It makes me feel pretty good. And I'm thinking, Wow, did those words really come out of my mouth? Where did they come from?

"When I first met George at Wayne's shop, I thought, 'What a total freak.' But then I realized that was just me judging people again. That's the way I was raised. I've been judging everybody all my life. George is just who he is. He's weird, but we're all weird. He's just George."

"He's just Meat, also," I say.

Eden smiles. "Actually, he kind of reminded me of you."

"That's a low blow."

"He's not trying to impress anybody. He taught me how to ride a motorcycle. And he took me to the Mud Club."

"Why did you go there?"

"To rub mud on my face like everybody else. Why else?"

"So why are you here? What are you looking for here?" I ask her.

"I can't explain that," she says. "But I can show you." She stands up. "If you don't mind taking a little hike."

Heads Up!

What do you think Eden has been doing while she's been away?

9

The Secret Place

***Ever find a spot where there's no one
to look at but yourself?***

Eden takes a trail that leads away from the beach. It heads through dense forest. It's all uphill.

We hike for ten or fifteen minutes. Then we reach the top. I feel like my gut is going to split. I'm huffing and puffing and sweating. Eden is hardly even out of breath.

We're in a small clearing. It's surrounded by trees. It's sheltered from the wind that comes from the ocean. It's peaceful and shady in here. The air is still. It's totally private.

We sit down on a big fallen tree. We look out through the trees at the ocean.

"Here we are," she says.

"Wow," I say.

"Yeah."

"What is this place?" I say. "A **launchpad** to Neptune?"

She laughs. "I like that."

Then she says, "I've come up to this place four times so far. I've sat up here all night, by myself. The first two times I got so scared, I thought I was going to die. The last two times, I stayed awake all night."

"What for?"

"When it gets dark, you realize you're stuck. You can't escape until daylight."

"So it's kind of like a test of courage or something?"

"That's part of it. More like a **rite of passage.**"

"What's supposed to happen?" I ask.

"Well, during the day, you sit here. You think. You sit very still. You get real bored and restless. You see eagles, maybe a deer. One time, I even saw a bear. Then night comes. It gets dark—

Heads Up!

Look up rite of passage *in the glossary.*
What do you think Eden means?

54

Eden shows Milo the place she goes to think.

and I mean *dark*. And you get really scared. You get **homesick** and lonely. And then you sort of let go of it. You lose yourself in the darkness. You blend in with everything around you. If you're lucky, the stars are out. You hear things, you see things. You see yourself. That's the beginning."

"Where do I sign up? I'm not kidding. I really do want to come up here and try it on my own. Maybe catch a **glimpse** of who the heck I am. It would be a start," I say.

We sit for a long time not saying anything.

Finally, I say, "You know, I should have said this a long time ago. I'm sorry for what I did in the hot tub."

"You don't have to apologize," she says. "You didn't do anything bad. You just . . . Well, I just wasn't expecting you to kiss me like that. It took me by surprise. We . . . we always seemed so much like a brother and sister. And then you wouldn't talk to me at all after that. I figured you thought I was a total prude. I thought you might have hated me."

"Actually, I was just really, really embarrassed. And I thought you hated me."

"Look, Milo," she says. "I don't know if this will surprise you or not. But I've always looked up to you. Always. Part of me has, that is. The good part of me. That's the part I'm trying to find."

Surprise me? How about knock me off the log? How about knock me right off the world?

Heads Up!

Now you know both sides of the story. How would you describe what happened to Milo and Eden's friendship?

10

Up and Running

Guess what? Eden's life wasn't the only thing that needed fixing.

After a while we hike back down to the cabin. Eden and I have a peanut butter sandwich. We sit around talking to Wayne and his sister. It starts to get late. So Wayne and I get on his motorcycle and ride back to Seattle.

It's nighttime when he drops me off at my car near his shop. "Let me know when you're ready to spend a few days at the cabin," he says.

"I'll do that. Thanks, Wayne."

When he's gone, I look at my watch. It's only ten-thirty. It's still Saturday night.

My car will not start. This is not a nice neighborhood to have a dead car. Ten minutes later, it still won't start. So I give up.

It's a long, scary walk to a pay phone. There are shadows in the doorways of the empty shops. I try not to look at them. I try not to look over my shoulder every minute. Finally, I get to the pay phone. I call a tow truck.

After I hang up, I put more coins in and call Mrs. Argo. I tell her about Eden. I try my best to answer all her questions. Then I go back to my car and wait for the tow truck.

The next Saturday, George and Lucy ride over to my house on George's motorcycle. My parents finally get to meet Lucy. I always thought they'd look at her like she's from outer space. They do, but I don't think Lucy minds. She knows the weirdness of parents.

My car has been sitting in the driveway all week, dead.

Heads Up!

Picture the conversation between Milo and Mrs. Argo. What questions do you think she asked? What do you think Milo told her?

George tells me to go and get whatever tools I own. He's going to introduce me to something called an engine. By the end of the day, the engine is running. The smoke is a lighter shade of purple.

The next Saturday, I'm lying in my driveway. I'm working on my car on my own. I've been working extra hours at my part-time job. I've been making trips to the junkyard for parts. I've bought some needed tools. They're scattered all around me. My hands and face are covered with oil and grease. I'm searching for my spark plug wrench.

I hear a motorcycle. I look up, expecting it to be George and Lucy. But it's just a single rider.

It's Eden.

She takes off her helmet and cuts the engine.

"You're home now?" I ask.

"I came back a couple days ago."

"You sort things out with your parents?"

"We're getting there. My school let me back in. But I won't be able to graduate with my class. I'm going to be up to my eyeballs in summer school. Keep that in mind if you ever decide to run off to a cabin."

"I'm going to do it after I graduate," I say. "I'm going back to that place. I'll need some help finding it again."

"I'll help you," she says.

I figure she means help me find the cabin. But she reaches down and picks something up. It's the spark plug wrench. She uses part of her shirt to wipe it off. Then she hands it to me.

Heads Up!

How has Eden changed? What detail at the very end gives you a clue?

Meet the Author

Randy Powell

"When I was in 8th grade I talked my parents into sending me to tennis camp. It cost them a lot more money than they could afford. But they said okay.

"While I was at the camp I met a girl my age. She was not only beautiful but very rich. She and I had a summer romance. Holding hands, we'd meet at midnight and walk under the rising moon.

"Well, um, actually, my roommate was the one who had the romance with her. He also had a father who happened to own a steel company. I could only imagine the fun he was having. I guess that's why I'm a writer—all that frustrated imagining I did."

Randy Powell must have been really frustrated back then because he's written a lot of books for teenagers. His titles include *My Underrated Year, Is Kissing a Girl Who Smokes Like Licking an Ashtray?,* and *Tribute to Another Dead Rock Star.*

Today, Randy lives with his wife and two boys in Seattle, Washington. You can check out his Web site at www.randypowell.com. Or send him an e-mail at randy@randypowell.com. He'd love to hear from you.

Glossary

achiever *(noun)* someone who has big goals for themselves and works hard to reach them (p. 24)

airbrush *(verb)* to paint over to hide anything that looks bad (p. 10)

awkwardly *(adverb)* uncomfortably (p. 47)

breakthrough *(noun)* an important step toward achieving something (p. 20)

chariot *(noun)* a small vehicle pulled by a horse in ancient times (p. 38)

driftwood *(noun)* wood that floats in the water or washes up on the shore (p. 48)

eventually *(adverb)* in time, after a while (p. 50)

flaw *(noun)* a fault or a weakness (p. 10)

fringe *(noun)* the edge; outside the norm (p. 10)

fume *(noun)* a bad-smelling smoke or gas (p. 8)

glimpse *(noun)* a quick look (p. 56)

hesitate *(verb)* to stop for a moment before doing something (p. 46)

homesick *(adjective)* missing your home (p. 56)

imitation *(noun)* a copy of someone or something else (p. 30)

launchpad *(noun)* a place where rockets or planes are launched (p. 54)

lunatic *(noun)* a crazy person (p. 19)

mutter *(verb)* to speak low and unclearly (p. 12)

programmed *(adjective)* instructed or trained to act in a certain way (p. 37)

rite of passage *(noun)* an experience that helps you grow up (p. 54)

ruddy *(adjective)* having a reddish color (p. 48)

saddlebag *(noun)* a pouch hanging from the seat of a motorcycle (p. 47)

snicker *(verb)* to laugh in a mean way (p. 16)

spitting image *(noun)* an exact duplicate or copy of someone else in looks (p. 6)

tempt *(verb)* to feel a strong urge to do something you're not supposed to (p. 33)

throb *(verb)* to beat or pound loudly (p. 22)

values *(noun)* a set of beliefs or ideas about what is most important (p. 50)